The Adventures of Andy and Nina

Pet Detectives

By KARD Publishing

This book is independently published.

First Edition, 2023

ISBN: 9798389771451

Contents

The Adventures of Andy and Nina: Pet Detectives

Introduction

• • •

Do you love pets? Do you have a passion for solving mysteries? Then you're in for a treat, because you're about to meet two of the best pet detectives in town: Andy and Nina!

Andy is a smart and spunky girl with a heart of gold. She loves nothing more than spending time with her furry friends and using her detective skills to solve puzzling cases.

Whether it's tracking down a lost dog or finding a missing cat, Andy is always up for a challenge. Her natural curiosity and sharp mind make her the perfect detective, and she's always ready to go the extra mile to help a pet in need.

Nina is Andy's faithful companion and sidekick, a lovable Boston Terrier with a nose for adventure. She's always by Andy's side, ready to sniff out clues and lend a helping paw. With her boundless energy and playful spirit, Nina is the perfect partner for Andy's detective work.

Together, Andy and Nina make an unbeatable team, solving mysteries and reuniting lost pets with their families. Whether they're chasing after a runaway guinea pig or investigating a case of pet theft, these two are always on the case! With their wit, bravery, and unbreakable bond, Andy and Nina are sure to capture the hearts of young readers everywhere.

So, are you ready to join Andy and Nina on their exciting adventures? Get ready for a wild ride, filled with twists, turns, and plenty of furry friends along the way. From the bustling city streets to the quiet suburbs, there's never a dull moment when these two are on the case. So, grab your magnifying glass and join Andy and Nina on their adventures. The pets of the world are counting on you!

The Case of the Missing Poodle

• • •

It was a sunny day in the neighborhood and Andy and Nina, pet detectives extraordinaire, were taking a break from their latest case by playing a game of catch in Andy's backyard. Andy threw the ball, and Nina ran after it with boundless energy, her tail wagging in excitement. Playing catch was one of Nina's favorite games, and she could go on for hours without ever getting tired.

Just as they were about to start another round of the game, Andy's phone rang. It was Mrs. Johnson, one of Andy's teachers from school who was worried sick about her missing poodle, Fluffy. Without hesitation, Andy and Nina leapt into action and took off.

Pedaling as fast as she could, Andy rode her bike to Mrs. Johnson's house with Nina running beside her. Mrs. Johnson had recently moved two blocks away from

Andy's house, so they were able to arrive quickly. When they arrived, they spoke with Mrs. Johnson, who told them that Fluffy had disappeared from her backyard.

Andy and Nina inspected the area, looking for clues that could lead them to find Fluffy. They found some paw prints, but they weren't sure if they belonged to Fluffy or another animal. They searched everywhere in the backyard and surrounding areas and found nothing.

4

Determined to find Fluffy, Andy and Nina decided to search the neighborhood. They walked through the streets, stopping to talk to people and ask if they had seen Fluffy or knew anything about his disappearance. No one had seen or heard anything suspicious.

The more they searched, the more frustrated Andy and Nina became. They knew they had to find Fluffy soon, or Mrs. Johnson would be devastated. With that in mind, they continued their search, determined to leave no stone unturned.

As they were walking through a nearby park, Nina suddenly stopped and barked excitedly. Andy followed her gaze and saw a small poodle that looked just like Fluffy being walked by an elderly woman.

"Excuse me, ma'am," Andy said, her voice quivering with excitement. "Is that your dog? We're looking for a lost poodle that looks just like him."

The woman looked surprised and said that she had found the dog wandering in the park and had decided to take care of him. Andy and Nina inspected the dog more closely, but their hopes were dashed when they realized that it wasn't Fluffy after all.

Disappointed but not deterred, they continued their search. They spent the next few hours searching every street, alleyway, and park in the neighborhood. Just as they were about to give up hope, they received a call from one of their friends who said that they had seen a poodle that looked like Fluffy being taken for a walk by a woman near the dog show happening nearby.

"Hey, Andy, I think I just saw Fluffy being walked near the dog show that's happening nearby," their friend said.

Andy and Nina thanked their friend and headed to the location. When they arrived, they saw a woman walking a poodle. Andy and Nina approached the woman and asked if the dog was Fluffy.

The woman looked surprised and said that she was taking care of the dog for a friend who was participating in the dog show. Andy and Nina asked for more details and learned that the dog show was happening nearby.

"We have to go to the dog show!" exclaimed Nina.

"Let's go!" replied Andy, determined to find Fluffy.

As they walked around the dog show, they saw many poodles, but none of them looked like Fluffy. Just as they were about to give up, they saw a poodle being held by a man who looked suspiciously like a man they had seen earlier in the park.

Andy and Nina exchanged a glance of recognition. They knew that the man holding the poodle was the same one they had seen earlier in the park. With renewed determination, they made their way over to him.

"Excuse me, sir," Andy said, trying to sound calm but failing. "That poodle you're holding, is he by any chance Fluffy?"

The man looked taken aback. "Uh, no, he's not Fluffy," he said, a little too quickly. But Andy and Nina were not easily fooled. They had been doing this for too long.

"Please, sir," Andy said, Nina barking at the man's feet. "We just want to find our friend's dog. It's important to her."

The man hesitated, then looked down at the poodle in his arms. "I did find him wandering around in the park," he admitted. "But I was planning to keep him. He's a prize-winning poodle, you know."

Andy and Nina exchanged a look of disbelief. How could someone be so heartless?

"That's not your decision to make," Andy said sternly. "You need to give Fluffy back to his owner. Now."

The man seemed to consider this for a moment, then sighed and handed Fluffy over to Andy and Nina. "Fine," he said gruffly. "But I want you to know that he's a valuable dog."

Andy and Nina didn't care about that. All they cared about was reuniting Fluffy with Mrs. Johnson. As they made their way back to Mrs. Johnson's house, they couldn't help but feel a sense of satisfaction. They had solved the case and brought Fluffy home safely. They knew that Mrs. Johnson would be overjoyed to see her beloved poodle again.

And they were right. As soon as they arrived at Mrs. Johnson's doorstep, Fluffy jumped out of Andy's arms and ran towards his owner, tail wagging furiously. Mrs. Johnson was beside herself with joy and gratitude.

"Thank you so much," she said, tears streaming down her face. "I don't know what I would have done without you two. You truly are pet detectives extraordinaire!"

Andy and Nina grinned at each other. They knew that this was just another job well done. Who knew what case they would solve next?

The Case of the Abandoned Pet Store

• • •

It was a cool late afternoon, and Andy and Nina were returning home from the park when they noticed something peculiar. The abandoned pet store on Main Street, which had been closed for years, appeared to have lights on inside. The windows were boarded up, but shadows could be seen moving around inside. Andy and Nina were curious and decided to investigate. As pet detectives, they were always on the lookout for a new case, and this one seemed to fall right into their lap.

They walked up to the front of the store and tried to peek through the boards. It was hard to see, but they could make out some cages and what looked like animal supplies. Their curiosity was piqued, and they knew they had to find out what was going on inside.

Andy and Nina walked around the back of the store, searching for any other entrance. They were surprised to find the back door slightly open. The two friends looked at each other, nodding silently in agreement. They pushed the door open slowly, trying not to make any noise. The room was dark, and they could hear the sound of animals scurrying about. Andy whispered to Nina, "We need to find a light switch." They searched the walls until

Nina found a light switch, and with a flick of her paw, the room was illuminated.

The room was filled with cages and animal supplies, just as they had suspected. But what caught their attention was the sound of muffled cries coming from one of the cages. They quickly made their way over to the source of the noise and found a small dog, huddled in the corner of a cage, whimpering softly.

"Oh, no," exclaimed Andy. "We need to get this dog out of here." Nina agreed and looked around for a key to unlock the cage. They found a set of keys hanging on a hook by the door and quickly tried them one by one until one of them finally opened the cage.

As they were taking the dog out of the cage, they heard footsteps coming from outside the store. They quickly hid behind a stack of crates and waited for the person to come inside. The door opened, and they saw a tall man with a hooded sweatshirt walk in. He walked over to the cage where the dog had been and saw that it was empty.

"What the-?" he muttered to himself. "Where did that dog go?" Andy and Nina looked at each other, knowing that they needed to get out of there fast. But as they tried to leave, they saw that the man had locked the back door. They were trapped.

"What are we going to do?" whispered Andy, fear evident in her voice. She thought for a moment and all of a sudden saw an opening through a broken window and then whispered, "We need to find a way to distract him and make a run for that window."

They looked around the room for anything they could use as a distraction. Andy spotted a bag of dog food and a water bowl on a nearby table. "I have an idea," she said, grabbing the bowl and filling it with water. She then tossed the water onto the man's back.

The man spun around, surprised, and Andy and Nina used that moment to run towards the window. They could hear the man's footsteps as he chased after them, but they were faster. They burst through the broken window and ran down the street, not stopping until they were sure they were safe.

Breathless, they took a moment to catch their breath before looking down at the small dog they had rescued.

He looked up at them with big brown eyes, wagging his tail gratefully. Andy and Nina knew they had to find the dog a home, and they decided to take him to the local animal shelter.

As they walked away from the abandoned pet store, Andy and Nina couldn't help but wonder who the man in the store was and what he was doing there. They knew that they had stumbled onto something big, and they were determined to find out what it was. They knew that this was just the beginning of their investigation.

Andy and Nina returned to the abandoned pet store, where they found other animals trapped inside, and noticed that most of them were exotic species, not sold in pet stores. They immediately notified the police and were able to have the owner of the pet store arrested.

Apparently, the owner of the abandoned pet store had recently began to use the location to sell and transport exotic animals illegally, but thanks to Andy and Nina's great detective work, it didn't last for long.

After the animals were rescued and taken to the animal shelter, Andy and Nina received a call from the town

Mayor who awarded them medals for their heroic efforts in rescuing the animals.

The next day, Andy and Nina were hailed as heroes by the people of the town. They received numerous thank you cards and even a cake from the local animal shelter. They were proud of their accomplishments, but they knew that their work was never done. They continued to keep an eye out for animals in need, always ready to help in any way they could.

The Quest of the Missing Parrot

• • •

Andy and Nina had been looking forward to their trip to the amusement park for weeks. They had planned the perfect day filled with thrilling rides, delicious treats, and plenty of laughter. As they stepped through the gates, the sounds and smells of the park washed over them, and their excitement soared. The sun shone brightly in the clear blue sky, and the park was bustling with people of all ages. The sight of roller coasters soaring through the air and colorful carnival games filled them with a sense of wonder and adventure. They took a deep breath and smiled at each other, knowing that they were in for an unforgettable day.

As they walked further into the park, Andy and Nina's eyes widened in awe. They saw the spinning teacups, the towering Ferris wheel, and the high-speed coaster that twisted and turned in the distance.

"Whoa, look at that coaster!" Andy exclaimed, pointing to the ride. "We have to go on that one!"

Nina barked in agreement and wagged her tail excitedly. As they made their way over to the coaster, they saw a group of people gathered around a stage. Curiosity piqued; they walked over to see what was happening.

"What's going on here?" Andy asked a woman in the crowd.

"A man's parrot has gone missing!" the woman replied. "He's offering a reward to anyone who can find it."

Nina's ears perked up at the mention of a missing pet. Excited, she barked. Andy nodded in agreement. "We're pet detectives. We can help find the missing parrot!"

As they approached the man, he explained that his parrot had gone missing from its cage and was nowhere to be found. He looked distraught and worried.

"Don't worry, we'll find your parrot!" Andy said, trying to reassure him.

Nina barked in agreement and sniffed around the area, trying to pick up any clues. The man explained that the parrot's name was Freddy, and he was a rare breed with brightly colored feathers and a unique circled pattern on his wings. He also mentioned that Freddy's favorite food was shredded carrots.

Andy and Nina exchanged a look. "We will get to the bottom of this," Andy said.

Nina barked and began to sniff around the area again, searching for any clues that could lead them to the missing parrot.

As Nina sniffed around the area, Andy began to question park visitors and employees. She asked if anyone had seen anyone suspiciously lurking around the bird exhibit earlier that day.

After speaking to a few people, Andy heard a familiar story. A man had been asking a lot of questions about the parrot and seemed overly interested in it.

"This could be a lead, Nina," Andy said, excitement rising in her voice. "Let's find this man and see what he knows."

They searched the park high and low trying to find clues that would help them identify the mysterious man and hopefully find the missing parrot.

As they gathered more information, they realized that the man had left a trail of clues behind. They found a feather on the ground near the parrot exhibit, right next to what appeared to be some kind of receipt or ticket stub.

The ticket stub had an unusual symbol on it, which they recognized as the logo of a local pet store.

"Let's go to the pet store, Nina," Andy said, feeling closer to finding Freddy. "Maybe the man left some clues there."

When they arrived at the pet store, they questioned the staff, who confirmed their suspicions. The suspicious man had been in the store earlier that day, asking about exotic birds.

"This man must have known what he was doing," Andy said, shaking her head. "He was trying to blend in and not raise suspicion."

Nina growled softly, sensing their mission was almost complete.

With the help of the pet store staff, Andy was able to review the security cameras and obtain the license plate number of the man's car which they immediately reported to the police.

Thanks to their detective work, the police were able to track down the thief and recover the stolen parrot. As they reunited Freddy the parrot with its owner, Andy and Nina couldn't help but feel a sense of pride and accomplishment.

"I knew we could do it, Nina," Andy said, beaming with pride.

Nina barked happily, wagging her tail in agreement.

As they left the park, they knew that they had not only helped someone in need, but they had also made a difference in the world. They had proven to themselves and others that they were more than just pet detectives, but heroes who were willing to go above and beyond to make a positive impact.

As they walked away from the park, Andy and Nina knew that they would never forget the quest for the lost parrot. They had learned valuable lessons about teamwork, perseverance, and the importance of never giving up on a mission.

"I can't wait to solve our next case, Nina," Andy said, looking down at her loyal companion.

Nina barked excitedly, eager to take on their next challenge as pet detectives.

The Museum Heist

• • •

Andy and Nina were walking through the city park, enjoying the warm summer day when they heard sirens in the distance. Their detective instincts immediately took them to follow the sounds until they reached the steps of the city's museum.

"What's happening?" asked Andy, her eyes wide as she watched the police officers and museum staff rush around the entrance.

"It looks like there's been a heist," replied a woman. Nina's nose twitched as she sniffed the air. "Do you smell something strange" asked Andy.

Andy and Nina approached the nearest officer and asked what was going on. The officer, a stern-looking man with a bushy mustache, told them that valuable paintings and artifacts had been stolen from the museum.

"We think the thief disabled the security system and broke in through the window," said the officer, pointing to the shattered glass on the ground.

Andy and Nina peered inside the museum and saw that the exhibition halls were empty. The paintings and artifacts that were usually on display were gone.

"How could someone do this?" wondered Andy. "And why?"

Nina nudged Andy with her nose, indicating that they should investigate. Andy nodded, and they walked towards the entrance of the museum. The museum staff and police officers were too busy to notice them slip inside.

The air inside the museum was cool and silent. Andy and Nina walked down the empty halls, looking for any clues that might help them solve the heist.

Suddenly, they heard a sound coming from the back of the museum. It sounded like someone was moving furniture.

Andy and Nina crept towards the source of the sound, trying not to make any noise. As they turned a corner, they saw a suspicious short figure darting towards the exit. They tried to follow it but couldn't keep up.

"Stop!" shouted Andy, but the suspicious short figure was too fast and by the time they reached the exit, was already out of sight.

All they could do was watch as the police officers scoured the area for any clues that could lead them to the thief.

Andy and Nina walked back to the police officers who were still investigating the crime scene. The museum staff was still in shock, and the police officers were trying to piece together what had happened.

As Andy and Nina approached the officers, they overheard them discussing that a group of monkeys was captured by a security camera from across the street and the possibility that they could have something to do with the heist. A group of monkeys had escaped from the zoo a few days ago.

"What do you mean, monkeys?" asked Andy, confused.

The police officer turned to her, "Yes, we received a call from the zookeepers that some of their monkeys had escaped from the zoo. We believe they may have something to do with the heist."

Andy and Nina exchanged a knowing look. They couldn't imagine how a group of monkeys could break into a museum and steal valuable paintings and artifacts.

"Are you sure it was the monkeys?" asked Nina, skeptically.

"Well, it's the only lead we have right now," replied the police officer.

Andy and Nina decided to visit the zoo to investigate the matter further. As they walked towards the zoo, they noticed several posters with pictures of the missing monkeys. They saw that the monkeys were from a rare species and that they needed to be returned to the zoo as soon as possible.

When they arrived at the zoo, they met with the zookeepers, who told them that the monkeys had been trained and were capable of performing complex tasks.

"We've been trying to find them for days, but we haven't had any luck," said one of the zookeepers.

Andy and Nina couldn't help but wonder if the monkeys were really responsible for the heist. They decided to search the zoo for any clues that could help them solve the case.

After several hours of searching, they found something unusual in the monkey exhibit. There was a small hole in the fence that surrounded the exhibit, and it looked like something had broken out.

"I don't think the monkeys escaped on their own," said Andy, examining the hole in the fence. "It looks like someone helped them."

Nina agreed, "And if someone helped them escape, they could have also used them to commit the heist."

Andy and Nina were determined to get to the bottom of this mystery. They knew they had to find the culprit who had stolen the monkeys and used them to commit the heist. The pet detectives had a new lead and were one step closer to solving the case.

They immediately returned to the museum to share their findings with the police officers and the museum staff. They told them about the possibility that someone had stolen the monkeys from the zoo to use them in the heist.

The police officers were intrigued by their theory and decided to investigate further. They asked Andy and Nina to assist them with the investigation since they were the ones who discovered the new lead.

The pet detectives were excited to help and began brainstorming ways to solve the case. They decided to start by interviewing the zookeepers to see if they had any information that could help them.

The zookeepers were cooperative and told them about a past employee who used to train the monkeys at the zoo. The employee had resigned several months ago under mysterious circumstances.

The police officers found out that the former employee's name was Mark and that he had left the zoo to start his own animal training business. They decided to pay him a visit and ask him some questions.

Mark denied any involvement in the heist and claimed that he had no idea where the monkeys were. However, the police officers noticed that Mark was nervous and seemed to be hiding something.

They decided to search his business and found a notebook with detailed instructions on how to disable the security system at the museum. They also found a map of the museum and a list of valuable artifacts that were stolen.

Mark finally confessed to his involvement in the heist. He had stolen the monkeys from the zoo and trained them to perform the heist. He had been planning the heist for months and had been waiting for the perfect opportunity.

The police officers were shocked by Mark's confession and asked him where the monkeys were. Mark told them that the monkeys were being kept safe and sound at a nearby location.

"We have to get those monkeys back to the zoo," said Andy.

Nina nodded in agreement,

The police officers immediately went to retrieve the monkeys and returned them to the zoo. The zookeepers were overjoyed to have the monkeys back and thanked Andy and Nina for their help in solving the case.

A few days later, the museum had restored all of the stolen paintings and artifacts. Andy and Nina went back to the museum to see them on display. They felt proud of themselves for their contribution to the case.

"I can't believe we solved the monkey heist," said Andy, beaming with pride.

The pet detective duo was ready for their next adventure.

The Haunted Doghouse

• • •

Andy and Nina were playing in their backyard when they noticed a moving truck parking next door. A family was moving in, and they had a dog with them. Andy's eyes lit up with excitement, "Hey, look at that! They have a dog!"

Nina's tail started wagging. "Let's go say hi!" said Andy.

They ran over to the fence and introduced themselves to the family. They met a young girl called Jackie and her cute dog Spots. They chatted for a while and learned that the family had just moved in from out of town.

"Nice to meet you! I'm Andy, and this is my best friend Nina," said Andy, extending her hand.

"We're pet detectives," said Nina, "We love solving mysteries and helping pets in need."

33

Jackie's eyes lit up, "Really? That's so cool! now that you mention it, there is something strange going on with Spots. He won't go near his doghouse since we moved here."

"His doghouse?" asked Andy.

"Yes," replied Jackie. "He used to love it at our old house, but now he avoids it like the plague. It's like he's afraid of it."

"Have you noticed anything strange about the doghouse?" asked Andy.

"Yes, I have," Jackie responded. "Sometimes I hear what sounds like scratching from the bottom and sometimes the doghouse moves a little on its own, It's really creepy."

"Scratching sounds and moving on its own?" repeated Andy, puzzled. "That definitely sounds strange."

Nina barked, "Looks like we have a mystery to solve!" said Andy.

Andy turned to Jackie, "Don't worry, we'll help you figure out what's going on with Spots' doghouse."

Jackie's face brightened, "Thank you so much! I really appreciate it."

With determination in their eyes, Andy and Nina headed to Jackie's backyard to start their investigation.

Andy and Nina started investigating Jackie's backyard for clues to help them figure out what was going on with Spots' doghouse. They searched high and low, but they couldn't find anything that would explain the strange occurrences.

"This is strange," said Andy. "There must be something going on."

Nina nodded, "I agree. We need to find some clues."

After searching for a while, they decided to put up a camera to record the doghouse and see if they could capture any strange activity. They set up the camera and waited patiently.

The next day, they reviewed the footage from the camera. At first, they didn't see anything unusual. But as they continued to watch, they noticed something strange. The doghouse appeared to be moving on its own, and they could hear the scratching sounds.

"Did you see that?" asked Nina, pointing to the screen.

"Yeah, I did," replied Andy. "It's like the doghouse is haunted or something."

Nina barked, "We need to investigate further!", replied Andy.

The duo continued to review the recordings and all of sudden were able to identify a small figure moving in and out from the side of the doghouse.

"Did you see that?" asked Andy this time, pointing to the screen. "That must be what's causing all of this". Nina wagging her tail in excitement. "We need to find out what that is," said Andy.

Nina nodded in agreement.

They decided to set up a trap near the doghouse to see if they could catch whatever was causing the strange occurrences.

Days went by, but nothing happened. They started to think that their plan had failed. That was until one morning when they heard a loud noise coming from Jackie's backyard.

"Did you hear that?" asked Andy.

Nina barked in response.

They ran to the backyard and found that the trap had been triggered. When they approached it, they saw a small animal scurrying away. It was too fast for them to see what it was.

"Whatever it was, it's causing all the commotion," said Andy.

Andy nodded, "We need to catch it and find out what it is."

Andy and Nina tried several attempts to catch the small figure that was causing all the mystery around Spots' doghouse, but they couldn't seem to catch it. They tried different baits and traps, but nothing seemed to work.

"This is so frustrating," said Andy. "We need to catch this thing and solve the mystery!"

Nina barked in agreement. Finally, after several attempts, they were able to catch the small figure. It turned out to be a groundhog! Andy and Nina couldn't believe it.

"A groundhog?" asked Andy. "How did it get in there?"

Nina added, "And how did it manage to get in and out without anyone noticing?"

They investigated further and found out that Jackie's parents didn't notice they had placed Spots' doghouse right on top of the hole to the groundhog's home. The groundhog was barely able to squeeze in and out, which was causing the scratching sounds and movement of the doghouse.

Realizing the cause of the mystery, Andy and Nina shared their findings with Jackie and her parents. They all laughed about it and were happy to have solved the mystery.

"I can't believe it was a groundhog all along!" said Jackie.

"I'm just glad we figured it out," replied her mom.

"And now, we know where to put Spots' doghouse," added her dad.

With the mystery solved and Spots' house relocated, Andy and Nina said their goodbyes to their new friends. They were proud of themselves for solving another case and were ready for their next adventure.

As they walked back to their house, Andy turned to Nina and said, "You know, being a pet detective is so much fun! I can't wait to see what kind of mystery we'll solve next."

Mystery at the Aquarium

• • •

The sun was shining brightly as Andy and Nina approached the entrance to the local aquarium. Today was the long-awaited school trip, and both Andy and Nina were excited to explore the wonders of the underwater world. Nina, wearing a special service dog vest, trotted happily alongside Andy, wagging her tail in anticipation.

As they passed through the gates, Andy's classmates buzzed with excitement around her. "I can't wait to see the sharks!" one boy exclaimed. "I heard there's a new jellyfish exhibit!" another girl chimed in. Andy's eyes sparkled as she took in the colorful displays and vibrant energy of the aquarium. She couldn't wait to learn more about the fascinating marine life and share the experience with her best friend, Nina.

Andy bent down to Nina and whispered into her ear, "This is going to be so much fun, Nina. I can't wait to see all the amazing creatures!" Nina barked softly in agreement, her brown eyes scanning the area as they ventured further into the aquarium.

As the group gathered around the large, central tank filled with an array of colorful fish, their teacher, Ms. Thompson, began to address the class. "Alright, everyone," she said, "We have a fun and educational day ahead of us. Make sure to pay attention to the exhibits and take notes for our follow-up assignment."

As Andy scribbled down some interesting facts about the sea creatures, she marveled at the diversity and beauty of the underwater world. Little did she know that her fun-filled day at the aquarium would soon take an unexpected turn.

Andy, Nina, and their classmates excitedly continued exploring the aquarium, visiting exhibits featuring cool sharks, amazing sea turtles, and schools of colorful fish. The excitement grew as they approached the most anticipated exhibit of the day: the rare Blue Moon Jellyfish.

As they got closer, they noticed a commotion up ahead. Aquarium staff huddled together, speaking in hushed tones, while curious visitors tried to see what was going on. Ms. Thompson led the group closer, her brow furrowed with concern.

Andy and Nina exchanged a puzzled look before moving through the crowd to find out what was happening. As they reached the front, they overheard one of the staff members say, "The Blue Moon Jellyfish is gone. It just vanished!"

The news spread quickly, and their classmates gasped with surprise. "How could it just disappear?" one boy asked. "Maybe it escaped!" a girl suggested.

Ms. Thompson quieted the class and turned to the nearest staff member. "What happened here? Is there anything we can do to help?"

The staff member, a tall woman with a worried expression, sighed. "We're not sure how this happened, but we appreciate your offer. For now, we ask that you continue with your tour while we try to figure this out."

As the class moved on to the next exhibit, Andy couldn't help but feel a burst of curiosity about the missing jellyfish. She whispered to Nina, "This could be our next case. What do you think?"

Nina barked softly in agreement, her keen senses already picking up on the mysterious atmosphere surrounding the disappearance.

With their detective instincts kicking in, Andy and Nina decided to keep a close eye on the situation.

They tried their best to focus on the rest of the school trip, but the mystery of the missing Blue Moon Jellyfish weighed on their minds. As they visited the remaining exhibits, they couldn't help but search for any possible clues.

Finally, the school trip came to an end, and the class headed back to school. However, Andy and Nina knew they had to return to the aquarium and assist with the case. The duo went back to the aquarium after school, determined to solve the mystery.

Upon their arrival, they interviewed several staff members. Andy approached one employee and asked, "Have you noticed anything unusual around the jellyfish exhibit   lately?"

The staff member thought for a moment before answering, "No, everything seemed normal until the jellyfish disappeared."

Andy and Nina searched for clues regarding the jellyfish's disappearance. Their investigation led them to a loose door lock near the exhibit, as if someone had tampered with it. Andy showed Nina the lock, saying, "This lock seems loose, like someone tried to break in."

Nina barked in agreement, and they continued their search.

With the help of the aquarium staff, they reviewed the security camera footage. Andy pointed out several possible suspects who were near the exhibit but couldn't find clear footage of anyone leaving with the jellyfish. Then, while reviewing the footage, Andy noticed a delivery person with a dark hat and sunglasses entering and leaving the jellyfish exhibit with what appeared to be a large box.

Andy turned to the staff and asked, "Were you expecting any deliveries today?"

A staff member replied, "No, we weren't. That's strange."

After identifying the delivery person suspect, they continued to investigate and managed to identify the delivery truck used from one of the outdoor security cameras. One of the aquarium staff members immediately recognized the truck, exclaiming, "I've seen that truck before! It's usually parked outside a warehouse near where I live!"

Andy and Nina became excited about this new lead and headed over to the warehouse the staff member had mentioned. They managed to fit through an open space in one of the rear fences and cautiously approached the warehouse to try to find the missing Blue Moon Jellyfish.

Peeking through one of the windows from the outside, they discovered something very surprising. Instead of finding the jellyfish, they stumbled upon a lot more. There were other animals as well, and it appeared to be a place where rare animals were collected and sold to the highest bidders.

Andy whispered to Nina, "I can't believe what we've found. We need to get help!" As they tried to leave, they were intercepted by a security guard who was watching over the warehouse. Andy and Nina attempted to make a run for it, but the guard caught them and took them inside the warehouse.

Locked in an office in the warehouse, Andy and Nina worried about how they were going to get out of this situation. Fortunately, Nina's sidekick skills and small size allowed her to squeeze out of one of the office windows. She then stealthily moved around the building and removed the lock from the other side of the door, freeing Andy.

The duo made a run for it and escaped before the guard noticed. They immediately went straight to the police station to report everything they had found and what had just happened. The police arrived quickly, rescued the animals, and put the people responsible behind bars.

In the end, Andy and Nina received credit from the local police department and the aquarium for solving the case. The chief of police praised them, saying, "You two have done an outstanding job! We couldn't have done it without you."

Their classmates were amazed by Andy and Nina's detective skills, and the duo eagerly awaited their next adventure, knowing that they could make a difference for animals in need. With their hearts full of pride and satisfaction, Andy and Nina knew that their bond and determination had once again helped them solve a thrilling case, proving that no mystery was too big for this unstoppable team.

The Green Valley National Park Crisis

• • •

The sun was shining brightly over Green Valley National Park, casting a warm glow over the lush green trees and vibrant wildflowers. The park was usually teeming with life, as animals roamed freely, and visitors came from all over to witness the beauty of nature. However, something was odd in the park, and the once lively atmosphere was now filled with concern and worry. The staff at the park had noticed that the animals were getting sick, and they couldn't pinpoint the cause. Desperate to find a solution, they decided to contact the town's famous pet detectives, Andy, and Nina.

Andy was sitting in her room, going over her notes from a previous case, while Nina dozed peacefully on the rug beside her. The phone rang, breaking the silence and jolting Nina awake. Andy answered the call and listened intently as the voice on the other end explained the troubling situation at the park.

"Hello, Andy? This is Ranger Smith from Green Valley National Park. We've heard about your impressive detective work, and we need your help. The animals in the park have been getting sick, and we can't figure out why. Can you and Nina come down to the park and help us?"

Andy's eyes widened with concern, and she quickly glanced at Nina, who was now fully awake and alert. "Of course, Ranger Smith. We'll be there as soon as we can."

After hanging up the phone, Andy grabbed her detective kit and called out to Nina, "Come on, girl. We've got a new case to solve!"

Nina barked excitedly, wagging her tail as they both headed out the door. As they made their way to the national park, Andy couldn't help but worry about the sick animals and the mysterious cause behind their illness. Little did she know that she and Nina were about to embark on one of their most challenging cases yet.

Andy and Nina arrived at Green Valley National Park, greeted by the worried park staff and Ranger Smith.

They were then led to the park's clinic, where several animals were being treated. "Thank you for coming, Andy and Nina. As you can see, the situation is quite serious," said Ranger Smith, pointing to the animals in the clinic. "We've tried everything we can think of but haven't been able to identify the cause of this."

Andy crouched down to examine a sick squirrel lying on a soft blanket, while Nina sniffed around the room, her ears perked up and alert. "Don't worry, Ranger Smith.

We'll do our best to figure out what's causing this," Andy reassured him.

As Andy and Nina investigated, they noticed that the sick animals had something in common: they all relied on the river running through the park as their primary water source. Andy remembered reading about similar cases where contaminated water had caused this type of illness in animals. She shared her thoughts with Ranger Smith.

"It could be the water supply," Andy suggested. "Have you noticed any unusual smells, tastes, or colors in the water?"

Ranger Smith scratched his head, deep in thought. "Not that I can think of. But now that you mention it, there have been some construction activities on privately-owned land upstream. I'm not sure if that's related, though."

With the suspicions of the river being contaminated due to the upstream construction, Andy and Nina decided to take water samples from various points along the river. They carefully collected the samples and sent them to the local lab for testing. Meanwhile, they continued interviewing the park staff and rangers to gather more information about the park and any recent changes in the area.

A few days later, Andy received a call from the lab with the test results. The lab technician explained that the water samples indeed contained dangerous levels of contamination, caused by a type of toxic waste. The contaminants were affecting the animals' health, just as Andy and Nina had suspected. With this new information, the duo knew they had to visit the construction site upstream to gather more evidence.

Andy and Nina arrived at the edge of the construction site, careful to remain hidden from view. They watched as large trucks moved in and out of the area, and workers busied themselves with various tasks. Their keen eyes soon spotted something alarming: barrels marked with hazardous waste symbols were being dumped into the river.

"We need to get evidence of this illegal dumping," whispered Andy, as Nina nodded in agreement.

They waited until nightfall, when the construction site was less active, and then sneaked closer to the riverbank. Using her smartphone, Andy took photos and videos of the barrels and the workers disposing of them. It was a risky mission, but they knew it was essential to stop the contamination and protect the animals in the park.

As they were about to leave the site, they heard voices approaching. Andy and Nina quickly hid behind a stack of unused lumber, their hearts pounding in their chests. They watched in silence as the workers walked by, completely unaware of their presence.

Once the coast was clear, Andy and Nina made a hasty retreat, relieved that they had gathered enough evidence to expose the illegal dumping. They reported their findings to Ranger Smith and the local authorities, providing them with the photos and videos they had captured.

Thanks to Andy and Nina's persistence and bravery, the developer responsible for the toxic waste dumping was brought to justice, and the construction site was shut down.

It took several days and a team of environmental specialists to clean and restore the river to its healthy state.

With the contamination stopped, the animals in Green Valley National Park began to recover and thrive once more. The park staff and the grateful community celebrated the young pet detectives for their invaluable help in solving the case and protecting the park's precious wildlife.

Andy and Nina had not only uncovered the source of the contamination but also played a crucial role in the river's restoration, ensuring a bright future for the animals and the park they called home.

A Stormy Vacation Rescue

• • •

The days leading up to their summer vacation were filled with anticipation and excitement. Andy and Nina, both looking forward to some well-deserved rest and relaxation, were at home counting down the days until their summer vacation trip.

Sitting on her bed with her loyal Boston Terrier, Nina, Andy was browsing through a colorful brochure about the island they would soon visit. "I can't wait to go snorkeling and see all the amazing fish," Andy said excitedly, pointing at a picture of a vibrant coral reef.

Nina wagged her tail enthusiastically, replying with a loud "bark".

Andy's younger brother, Ben, burst into the room, waving a zip-lining brochure. "This is going to be so much fun! I can't believe we're finally going on vacation."

Their mom called from downstairs, "Kids, come help pack your suitcases. We don't want to forget anything important!"

Andy, Nina, and Ben rushed downstairs to assist with the packing, eagerly discussing their plans for the upcoming vacation. Little did they know that their summer vacation would turn into an unforgettable adventure.

As the day of their departure arrived, Andy and Nina eagerly stared out the window as the airplane descended towards the beautiful Caribbean Island. The vibrant blue ocean and sandy beaches seemed to call their names.

As the plane touched down, Andy's parents led the family to a stunning hotel that overlooked the beach. "This place is amazing!" Andy exclaimed, her eyes wide with excitement.

Nina wagged her tail in agreement, sniffing the salty air as they walked towards the hotel entrance.

The hotel manager greeted them with a warm smile. "Welcome to our island paradise! I hope you enjoy your stay."

"Thank you," Andy's mom replied. "We're looking forward to exploring the island and taking a break from our daily routines."

Over dinner that night, the family discussed the various activities they wanted to do during their vacation. Andy couldn't wait to go snorkeling, while her younger brother, Ben, was excited about the zip-lining tour.

As they finished eating, they overheard some locals talking about an approaching hurricane. Concerned, Andy's dad asked the hotel manager, "Excuse me, is there a hurricane headed this way?"

The manager nodded gravely. "Yes, there's a storm system developing. It's still uncertain if it'll hit the island directly, it is not common to see this time of year, but we're monitoring the situation closely."

Andy and her family exchanged worried glances, but decided to make the most of their vacation while they could.

The next day, Andy and Nina explored the island together, enjoying the warm sunshine and crystal-clear water. As they walked through the town, they couldn't help but notice the large number of stray dogs and cats roaming the streets.

"Look, Nina," Andy said softly, "There are so many stray animals here. It's so sad."

Nina whined in agreement, her ears drooping.

As the days passed, the news of the hurricane grew more concerning, and it seemed increasingly likely that it would hit the island. Andy and Nina began to worry about all the stray animals they saw in the town. Andy said to Nina with a worried tone, "Where will these animals take shelter during the storm? We need to do something".

Determined to help, Andy and Nina approached the local authorities to inquire about their plans to rescue the stray animals before the storm. They found Officer Gomez, a friendly and concerned animal control officer, at the town hall.

"Officer Gomez," Andy asked, "what are your plans to help the stray animals on the island before the hurricane hits?"

Officer Gomez sighed, "We're trying our best, but we're overwhelmed with work and short-staffed. We could use all the help we can get."

Andy and Nina exchanged a glance before volunteering, "We're here to help. We'll do whatever we can to make sure the animals are safe before the storm hits."

Officer Gomez smiled gratefully, "Thank you, kids. Your help will make a big difference."

Over the next day, Andy and Nina worked tirelessly with Officer Gomez and the local volunteers, going door-to-door, searching alleyways and under bushes, trying to locate and shelter the stray animals. Nina's keen senses were invaluable, her sharp ears and sensitive nose helping them locate most of the frightened animals.

As the wind began to pick up and the first raindrops fell, Andy and Nina managed to find shelter for most of the animals. However, they knew that not all of them were safe, and there was a sense of unease in their hearts as they thought about the rescue mission that lay ahead after the hurricane passed. The young detectives braced themselves with their family, determined to face the storm and help as many animals as possible.

The storm raged through the night, the howling wind and lashing rain creating a terrifying symphony. Andy, Nina, and their family huddled together in the hotel, grateful for the sturdy building that sheltered them. When dawn broke, the hurricane had passed, leaving a trail of destruction in its wake.

Andy and Nina peered out the hotel window, surveying the damage. They were relieved to see that the hotel and its guests were safe, but the town and surrounding areas had not fared as well. Their hearts went out to the stray animals they knew must be out there, in need of help.

Determined to continue their rescue mission, Andy and Nina ventured into the devastated town. Debris littered the streets, trees had fallen, and some wooden structures had collapsed. The young detectives' eyes scanned the area, searching for any animals that needed their help.

Their first rescue came at a flooded river, where they spotted a frightened dog struggling against the strong current. "Nina, look! We need to help that dog!" Andy cried out. Nina nodded, and they sprang into action, using a long branch to reach the desperate animal. "Hold on, buddy!" Andy shouted, reaching out with the branch. With great effort and teamwork, they managed to pull the dog to safety.

Their next rescue took them to a collapsed structure, where they heard faint meows coming from within the rubble. "I hear them, Nina! They must be trapped in there," Andy said anxiously. Carefully, Andy and Nina began to move the debris, trying to reach the trapped cats. With persistence and patience, they eventually uncovered a small pocket where several cats huddled together, frightened but unharmed. "It's okay, little ones. We're here to help," Nina whispered gently as she helped the cats out.

Throughout the day, Andy and Nina continued their brave efforts, rescuing more animals affected by the storm. "We're doing great, Nina. We're making a difference," Andy encouraged. Thankfully, none were harmed, and the young duo was happy they could help.

As the sun began to set, Andy and Nina returned to their hotel, tired but fulfilled. They knew they had played a crucial role in helping the island's animals survive the storm, and their hearts swelled with pride. This stormy vacation had turned into one of their most exciting and rewarding adventures as pet detectives.

Andy and Nina's family, still overwhelmed and frustrated by the situation, were proud and amazed by their accomplishment.

In the days that followed, Andy and Nina continued to assist in the island's recovery, and they formed strong bonds with the local community members who were also helping. Their tireless work and love for animals touched the hearts of the locals, who admired the young detectives' dedication.

One afternoon, as they were helping to repair a damaged shelter, Andy and Nina met Maria, the head of the island's animal rescue organization. Maria, impressed by their passion, asked the young detectives for their thoughts on how to improve the island's stray animal programs.

"Well, you could set up more feeding stations and shelters for the animals," Andy suggested. "That way, they'll have a safe place to go when there's bad weather."

She also suggested, "And maybe you could organize more community events to raise awareness about the importance of adopting and caring for strays. That way, more people will be involved in helping the animals."

Maria listened intently, nodding in agreement. "Those are excellent ideas. Thank you, Andy, and Nina. Your help and insights have been invaluable."

Finally, the day arrived for Andy, Nina, and their family to return home. They had experienced an unforgettable vacation, full of adventure, new friendships, and, of course, the incredible rescue missions.

As they boarded the plane, Andy's father put his arm around her and Nina. "You two really made a difference here. I'm so proud of both of you," he said, his eyes shining with admiration. "Remember, even when you're faced with difficult situations, you can always find a way to help others and make a positive impact."

Andy smiled while Nina wagged her tail excitedly, their hearts full of pride and gratitude. They knew that their summer vacation would always hold a special place in their memories, not just because of the beautiful

Caribbean Island, but because of the incredible rescue adventure and the inspiring friendships they had formed. This trip taught them that no matter the circumstances, there is always a way to make a difference and help others.

The Dog Show Mystery

• • •

The annual pet show had finally arrived in town, and the atmosphere was buzzing with excitement. Colorful banners fluttered in the breeze, and the air was filled with laughter and barks of anticipation. This three-day event was the highlight of the year for both pets and their owners, as they showcased their talents and competed for the top titles.

As the first day of the pet show unfolded, everyone's excitement turned into confusion and concern. Something strange was happening to some of the competing dogs. During their performances, several dogs started acting out of character, as if they were disturbed by something. They whimpered, cowered, and refused to follow their owners' commands.

"What's going on with some of the dogs?" one spectator whispered to another.

"I have no idea," the other replied, shaking their head. "They were all fine during the rehearsals."

The dog show staff tried their best to figure out what was causing the disturbance, but they couldn't come up with any answers. The show's organizer, Mr. Thompson, scratched his head in frustration.

"We can't have this continue," he said to his assistant. "We need to find out what's happening before the show is ruined."

His assistant nodded. "You're right, sir. It's time to call in the experts: Andy and Nina, the town's pet detectives."

With no time to waste, Mr. Thompson picked up his phone and dialed the number for the duo. The phone rang a few times before Andy picked up.

"Hello, Andy speaking."

"Ah, Andy, it's Mr. Thompson from the pet show. We need your help! Something strange is going on with the contestants, and we can't figure out what's causing it. Can you and Nina come down to investigate?"

Andy glanced at Nina, who was already wagging her tail excitedly. "Of course, Mr. Thompson. We'll be there right away."

With determination in their eyes, Andy and Nina set off to the pet show, ready to solve the mystery.

Andy and Nina arrived at the bustling pet show, ready to dive into their investigation. As they made their way through the crowd, they could sense the confusion and concern among the participants and spectators. They knew they had to act fast to save the show.

"Let's start by talking to the owners of the affected dogs," Andy suggested, scanning the area for clues.

Nina barked in agreement, and the duo approached a worried-looking woman with a Scottish Terrier. The woman was trying to calm her dog down, but the poor terrier seemed quite agitated.

"Excuse me, ma'am," Andy said gently, "We're Andy and Nina, the pet detectives. We're here to help figure out what's bothering the dogs. Could you tell us what happened during your performance?"

The woman looked relieved to see them. "Oh, thank goodness you're here! My Scottie, Angus, was doing just fine during the rehearsals, but when we stepped onto the stage, he suddenly started whining and wouldn't follow any of my commands. It was like he was hearing something that I couldn't."

Andy and Nina exchanged glances. This seemed to be a common theme among the affected dogs.

"Thank you for sharing," Andy said. "We'll do our best to get to the bottom of this."

As they continued to interview more dog owners, they found that all the stories were strikingly similar. Every terrier had been perfectly fine during rehearsals but had become unresponsive or agitated during the actual show.

"Looks like we've found our connection, Nina," Andy said thoughtfully. "All the affected dogs are in the terrier category. We need to figure out what's causing this."

Nina nodded, her eyes focused and determined.

"We should attend the next terrier show," Andy suggested. "Maybe we can find more clues during the performance."

As they found their seats and waited for the show to begin, Andy reviewed her notes, searching for any possible leads. As soon as the terrier category began their performances, the strange behavior started again. To their surprise, Nina suddenly whimpered and began pawing at her ears.

"Nina, are you okay?" Andy asked, concerned.

Nina looked at her young owner, her eyes filled with distress. It was clear that whatever was affecting the other terriers was also bothering her.

Andy's eyes widened as she realized the significance of what was happening. "Nina, you're reacting just like the other terriers. Whatever is causing this, you can hear it too!"

Andy and Nina knew they needed more information to understand what was affecting the terriers. They decided to visit a well-respected dog trainer in town, Mrs. Martinez, hoping she could provide some insights.

As they approached Mrs. Martinez's training center, the sounds of dogs barking and people giving commands filled the air. The duo found Mrs. Martinez instructing a class on agility exercises.

"Mrs. Martinez?" Andy called out, waiting for a break in the action.

The dog trainer turned and smiled warmly. "Hello, Andy and Nina! What brings you here today?"

Andy explained the situation at the pet show, describing the strange behavior of the terriers and Nina's reaction during the performance.

Mrs. Martinez frowned, deep in thought. "Hmm, it sounds like the dogs might be reacting to a high-frequency sound that only they can hear. In fact, there's a rare type of whistle that's said to only be heard by terriers."

"A whistle?" Andy asked, intrigued. "Do you think someone could be using it to sabotage the dog show?"

"It's certainly possible," Mrs. Martinez replied. "But it's important to note that this type of whistle isn't sold in stores. Someone would have to make it themselves."

Andy and Nina exchanged a determined glance. They now had a lead and a possible motive. With renewed energy, they set out to find the source of the mysterious whistle.

As they walked through the town, Andy mused aloud, "If the whistle isn't sold in stores, then we need to find someone who knows how to make them. Maybe there's a connection between the whistle maker and the pet show."

Nina barked in agreement, her eyes scanning their surroundings for any potential clues.

Their search led them to the local library, where they spent hours researching whistles and their makers.

Finally, they stumbled upon a newspaper article about a local craftsman named Mr. Caldwell, who was known for creating unique and specialized whistles. The article also included a picture of Mr. Caldwell.

"We've got to find Mr. Caldwell and ask him about the terrier whistle," Andy declared, excitement in her voice.

Suddenly, Nina let out a low growl, her eyes fixed on the picture of Mr. Caldwell. Andy looked down at the photo and gasped. "Nina, you're right! We've seen him before. I think he was at the dog show!"

"This changes everything, Nina," Andy said, her eyes widening in disbelief. "We need to go back to the dog show and keep an eye on Mr. Caldwell."

With a new lead to follow, Andy and Nina hurried back to the pet show, eager to find the source of the mysterious whistle and uncover the truth.

Andy and Nina arrived back at the bustling pet show, determined to keep a close eye on Mr. Caldwell, the whistle maker. They knew they needed to catch him in the act to prove he was responsible for the strange behavior of the terriers.

"We need to stay close and watch his every move," Andy whispered to Nina. "We have to catch him using the whistle."

Nina barked in agreement, and the duo discreetly searched for Mr. Caldwell among the crowd. As they spotted him near the stage, they maintained a safe distance so as not to raise suspicion.

As the next terrier performance began, Andy and Nina watched Mr. Caldwell intently, waiting for any sign of mischief. The terriers took the stage, and the audience eagerly anticipated their performance.

As the performance progressed, the terriers suddenly began acting strangely again. Andy noticed Mr. Caldwell subtly raising the small whistle to his lips and discreetly blowing into it.

"Nina, look!" she whispered, pointing to Mr. Caldwell. "He's up to something!"

With their suspect in sight, Andy and Nina continued to shadow Mr. Caldwell, ready to expose his sabotage. When the terriers on stage seemed even more disturbed, Andy decided it was time to confront him.

"Gotcha!" Andy shouted, stepping forward and pointing at Mr. Caldwell. "You've been using that whistle to sabotage the dog show!"

The crowd gasped, and all eyes turned to Mr. Caldwell, who stood frozen with the whistle still pressed to his lips. The jig was up, and Andy and Nina had successfully cracked the case.

As the pet show staff escorted Mr. Caldwell away, Andy couldn't help but wonder why he would want to sabotage the dog show in the first place. It just didn't make any sense.

"Why did you do it, Mr. Caldwell?" Andy asked, filled with curiosity.

Mr. Caldwell sighed, his shoulders slumping in defeat. "I used to be a big supporter of the dog show, and I worked on the staff for many years. But the new coordinator decided to bring in staff from out of town and removed me from my position. I felt hurt and betrayed, so I wanted to get back at them by sabotaging the show."

The other participants and spectators, while disappointed in Mr. Caldwell's actions, could understand the pain behind his motive. Andy took this opportunity to share a lesson with everyone present.

"Mr. Caldwell, we all experience difficult times and face unfair situations in life, but it's important not to act in a vengeful way. Instead, we should always love and respect each other, no matter what. Acting out of anger only causes more harm and doesn't solve anything."

Mr. Caldwell nodded, realizing the truth in Andy's words. "You're right, young lady. I let my hurt feelings get the best of me, and I made a terrible mistake. I promise to do better and make amends for my actions."

With another mystery solved and a very important lesson learned, Andy and Nina were excited about what to expect next.

The Purr-fect Rescue

• • •

P aws & Whiskers Pet Hotel was the epitome of luxury for pets. Nestled in a quiet corner of town, the boutique-style establishment boasted an elegant interior, top-notch amenities, and a staff that catered to every whim of its furry clientele. The pet hotel was famous for pampering pets like royalty, and that's why Mrs. Pennington, a wealthy cat owner, didn't hesitate to leave her adored Persian cat, Mr. Fluffles, in their care whenever she needed to travel.

One day, Mrs. Pennington received a last-minute call to attend a business meeting out of town. With Mr. Fluffles in her arms, she rushed into the lavish lobby of Paws & Whiskers, where the receptionist greeted her with a warm smile.

"Welcome back, Mrs. Pennington," she said cheerfully. "We'll take excellent care of Mr. Fluffles during your trip."

Three days later, Mrs. Pennington returned, eager to reunite with her beloved feline companion. Little did she know, her world was about to be turned upside down.

As the receptionist went to fetch Mr. Fluffles, her expression changed from cheerful to worried. "Mrs. Pennington, I'm afraid we can't seem to find Mr. Fluffles," she said, her voice trembling.

"What do you mean you can't find him?" Mrs. Pennington exclaimed, her eyes wide with fear and disbelief.

Panic set in as the entire staff searched the pet hotel from top to bottom, but Mr. Fluffles was nowhere to be found. Desperate for help, the pet hotel owner, Mr. Thompson, picked up the phone and dialed a number he hoped would bring some much-needed assistance.

"Hello, Andy? This is Mr. Thompson from Paws & Whiskers Pet Hotel. We have a situation here, and we need your help," he explained, his voice filled with urgency. "Can you and Nina come right away?"

Andy's voice was confident and reassuring on the other end of the line. "Of course, Mr. Thompson. Nina and I will be there as soon as possible."

When Andy and her trusty Boston Terrier sidekick, Nina, arrived at Paws & Whiskers Pet Hotel, they were greeted by a worried Mr. Thompson.

"Thank you both for coming so quickly," he said, shaking Andy's hand. "We're at a complete loss. Mr. Fluffles just vanished into thin air."

Andy nodded, her eyes scanning the luxurious surroundings. "Don't worry, Mr. Thompson. Nina and I will do our best to find Mr. Fluffles and bring him back safely."

Nina wagged her tail, eager to start investigating. Together, they began to examine the pet hotel. They questioned the staff and checked Mr. Fluffles' suite for any signs of forced entry or escape routes. Everything seemed to be in perfect order, making the disappearance even more puzzling.

"Nina, we need to think outside the box," Andy said, stroking her chin. "There's got to be something we're missing."

Nina sniffed the air, her ears perked up, and she trotted towards the security room. Andy followed her, curious about what her canine companion had picked up on.

Inside the security room, they found the video monitors displaying live footage from various cameras placed throughout the hotel. Andy asked the security guard on duty if they could review the footage from the past few days. The guard hesitated, then sheepishly admitted that all footage had been mysteriously erased during the time of Mr. Fluffles' disappearance.

Andy's eyes narrowed. "This makes me think it could be an inside job. Someone might be trying to cover their tracks."

Nina barked in agreement, and they decided to take a closer look at the hotel staff. They interviewed each member, searching for any inconsistencies in their stories or signs of guilt. Everyone seemed genuinely concerned about the missing cat and claimed to know nothing about his disappearance.

Frustrated by the lack of solid leads, Andy and Nina decided to regroup and plan their next move. Just as they were about to leave the hotel, Mrs. Pennington received a mysterious letter. The letter claimed that Mr. Fluffles had been kidnapped, and the person responsible demanded a large sum of money for his safe return.

The stakes had suddenly risen, and Andy and Nina knew they had to act fast. With a determined look on her face, Andy turned to Nina. "We have a kidnapping on our hands. Let's get to work and find Mr. Fluffles before it's too late."

Andy and Nina arrived at Mrs. Pennington's lavish home to examine the ransom letter. The distraught cat owner handed over the letter, tears streaming down her face. "Please find Mr. Fluffles," she pleaded. "He means everything to me."

Andy gently patted Mrs. Pennington's hand. "We'll do everything we can to bring him back home safely, I promise."

While Andy carefully inspected the letter, Nina sniffed it, her nose twitching. Suddenly, her ears perked up, and she let out an excited bark. Andy looked at her trusty sidekick with a curious expression. "What is it, Nina? Did you find something?"

Nina continued to sniff the letter, and then bolted towards the door, signaling that she had picked up a scent. Andy quickly followed her, and together they traced the scent through the streets of the town.

As they followed the trail, Andy couldn't help but wonder where it was leading them. The scent seemed to be getting stronger, and Nina became more determined with each step. Finally, they found themselves in front of a small pizza shop.

Andy raised an eyebrow, puzzled. "A pizza shop, Nina? It's not a time for pizza. Are you sure this is where the scent leads?"

Nina barked confidently and wagged her tail. Trusting her canine companion's instincts, Andy decided to enter the pizza shop to see if anyone inside could provide any information about the mysterious ransom letter.

Once inside, Nina immediately began barking at one of the staff members behind the counter. The young man looked nervous, and beads of sweat formed on his forehead.

Andy approached the counter, doing her best to appear calm and friendly. "Hello, my name is Andy, and this is my partner, Nina. We're investigating a missing cat, and we believe that someone from this pizza shop might be involved. Have you seen anything suspicious lately?"

The young man swallowed hard, his eyes darting back and forth. "N-no, I haven't seen anything. I don't know anything about a missing cat."

Andy and Nina exchanged a knowing glance. They could tell that something was off, and they decided to keep a close eye on the pizza shop. They hid in a nearby alley, watching the shop for any signs of suspicious activity.

As night fell, Andy and Nina, determined that there was something suspicious with the pizza shop, decided to enter the shop through a rear window to search for the missing cat. They moved cautiously, trying not to alert anyone to their presence. After a thorough search, they found no trace of Mr. Fluffles, but they remained suspicious.

Unwilling to give up, they decided to return the next morning, which was the day the ransom had been scheduled to be exchanged, to see if someone left the shop with the cat. Andy and Nina hid in the same alley as before, keeping a close eye on the shop's entrance.

To their surprise, they saw one of the staff members from the pet hotel enter the pizza shop. This further confirmed their suspicions about the shop's involvement in the catnapping.

Their hearts raced as they continued to wait and watch. After what felt like an eternity, they saw someone exit the shop carrying what appeared to be a small cage with a cat inside. Andy and Nina exchanged excited glances – they couldn't believe their eyes.

"This has to be Mr. Fluffles!" Andy whispered to Nina, trying to contain her excitement. "We need to follow them and find a way to rescue him."

The two pet detectives cautiously trailed the person carrying the cage, ready to leap into action when the moment was right. The stakes were high, but they were more determined than ever to solve the case and reunite Mr. Fluffles with his loving owner.

Andy and Nina followed the person carrying the cage with Mr. Fluffles inside, keeping a safe distance so as not to be noticed. As they trailed the kidnapper, Andy tried to come up with a plan to create a diversion and rescue the cat.

"Okay, Nina," Andy whispered, "We need to create a distraction so that I can get close enough to grab the cage."

Nina wagged her tail in agreement, her eyes filled with determination.

They continued to follow the kidnapper until he reached a busy street. Andy spotted a group of pigeons pecking at some crumbs on the sidewalk. She quickly took a handful of pebbles from the ground and whispered to Nina, "When I throw these pebbles at the pigeons, they'll fly up and cause a commotion. That should be enough to distract the kidnapper. Then, you'll wrap this rope around his legs while I grab the cage. Ready?"

Nina barked softly, and Andy knew she was ready for action.

Andy hurled the pebbles at the pigeons, and as she had predicted, the birds took flight, flapping their wings and squawking loudly. The sudden commotion caught the attention of the kidnapper, who momentarily looked away from the cage.

Seizing the opportunity, Nina sprang into action. She held one end of the rope in her teeth and ran circles around the kidnapper, swiftly wrapping the rope around his legs. Just as Nina finished, the kidnapper lost his balance and tumbled to the ground.

Andy dashed forward, snatched the pet cage with Mr. Fluffles inside, and made a run for it. Nina quickly followed, her tail wagging triumphantly.

As they ran, Andy couldn't help but feel proud of their teamwork. Together, they had managed to outsmart the kidnapper and rescue Mr. Fluffles. Now all that was left was to return the cat to its relieved owner and let the authorities deal with the criminals.

Andy and Nina raced back to Mrs. Pennington's home, the pet cage in tow. As they approached her front door, they could hear the worried owner pacing inside.

Andy knocked on the door, and Mrs. Pennington swung it open, her eyes wide with concern. "Andy, Nina, did you...?" she trailed off when she saw the pet cage in Andy's hands.

"Mrs. Pennington, we found Mr. Fluffles!" Andy exclaimed, and Nina wagged her tail proudly. The wealthy cat owner gasped in relief, her eyes filling with tears of joy. She reached into the cage and gently scooped out her beloved cat, cradling him in her arms.

"Thank you so much, Andy and Nina! I don't know what I would have done without you," Mrs. Pennington said, her voice trembling with gratitude. "Please, let me give you a reward for your incredible detective work."

Andy hesitated, but Mrs. Pennington insisted, handing them a generous check. "Use this to help other animals in need," she said.

Andy and Nina exchanged a knowing look, aware that this money would help them continue their work as pet detectives. As they left Mrs. Pennington's home, they couldn't help but reflect on the impact their detective skills had on the animals they had helped so far.

"This is just the beginning, Nina," Andy said, looking at her furry partner. "We're going to keep growing, solving more complex cases, and making a difference for animals everywhere."

Nina barked in agreement, her eyes shining with determination. Together, they walked off into the sunset, ready for whatever new challenges and mysteries awaited on their next adventures as pet detectives.

THANK YOU!

Dear Reader,

Thank you so much for joining Andy and Nina on their thrilling adventures throughout this series! We hope you've enjoyed their incredible journey as much as we have.

As we reach the end of this book, we'd like to kindly ask you to share your thoughts by leaving a review on Amazon.

Your feedback is important to us and helps other readers discover the exciting world of Andy and Nina, Pet Detectives.

Thank you once again for embarking on this adventure with Andy and Nina. Your enthusiasm for their stories encourages us to continue creating captivating tales for readers like you.

Happy reading!

Made in the USA
Monee, IL
24 April 2023

32336870R00056